W9-BGX-183

Ghastly Ghosts

Teresa Bateman
illustrated by Ken Lamug

Albert Whitman & Company
Chicago, Illinois

A story to shiver your spine and chill your toes for
Oliver, Matthew, Bennett, and Charlie—TB

For my sister, Che, whose warmth
will never fade—KL

Library of Congress Cataloging-in-Publication data is on file with the publisher.

First published in the United States of America in 2019 by Albert Whitman & Company
ISBN 978-0-8075-2864-8 (hardcover)
ISBN 978-0-8075-2865-5 (ebook)

Printed in China
10 9 8 7 6 5 4 3 2 1 WKT 24 23 22 21 20 19

Design by Aphee Messer

For more information about Albert Whitman & Company,
visit our website at www.albertwhitman.com.

100 Years of Albert Whitman & Company
Celebrate with us in 2019!

When Old Dave's uncle passed away,
he left a place for Dave to stay—
A cottage on a lonely height,
far from friends and city lights.

Home Sweet Home

A door hinge *squeeeeeaked* when Dave moved in.

He didn't mind, just gave a grin,
and got some oil to fix the door.
"It's just some rust," he said. "No more."
Unpacking all his boxes, he
heard footsteps where none ought to be—
from attic floors above his head.
"I'm sure it's mice," is what he said.

"Some mice around is fine with me.
I think I'd like the company.
It's not much fun to be alone."

Then from the bathroom came a *MOOOAN.*

"The pipes are old, like me," said Dave.
"I hope they work—I need a shave.
These whiskers don't look good on me.
Not that there's anyone to see."

Then from the cellar came a *waailll*
that made Dave start, and then turn pale.

He laughed. "Must be a broken pane.
That's easy enough to explain."

He settled in and tried to rest.
He heard odd sounds,
yet did his best
to act as if he didn't care.
Still, he felt lonely living there.

A storm that night turned rain to ice.
Dave said aloud, “It would be nice—
indeed, I’d say that I’d rejoice—
if I could hear another voice.”

The lonely cottage creaked and swayed.
Old Dave rocked back, his fiddle played.
The wind blew wild and something said,

"Ghastly ghosts in the old coal shed!"

He paused and gave his head a shake.
Was he asleep or still awake?

"Never mind what I just said,
I'd like a *living* voice, not dead."
Then something even louder said,

**"Ghastly ghosts
in the old coal shed!"**

Wind whistled on the windowsill.
Old Dave began to feel a chill.

"The fire's getting low, no doubt,
or maybe it's about gone out.
I'll poke it up then go to bed."

Yet voices even louder said,
"Ghastly ghosts in the old coal shed!"

Dave grabbed the poker. His desire!
To stir things up, restart the fire.
But with a sinking of his soul,
he saw the hearth was out of coal.

Again the choir, much louder, said,
"Ghastly ghosts in the old coal shed!"

The wind was ice. The pipes would freeze.
The house grew colder by degrees.
There was a chore Dave had to do—
Fetch coal to see the cold night through.

He got his boots, gloves, scarf, and hat,
shrugged on his coat and that was that.

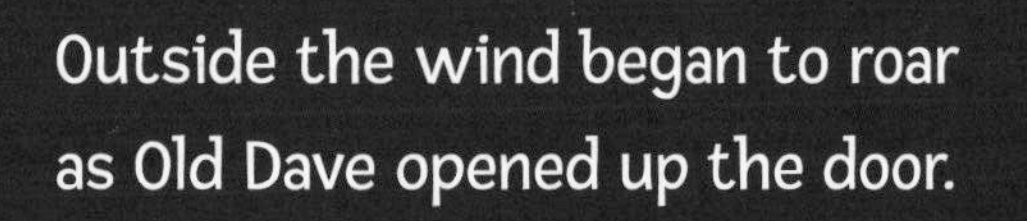

Outside the wind began to roar
as Old Dave opened up the door.

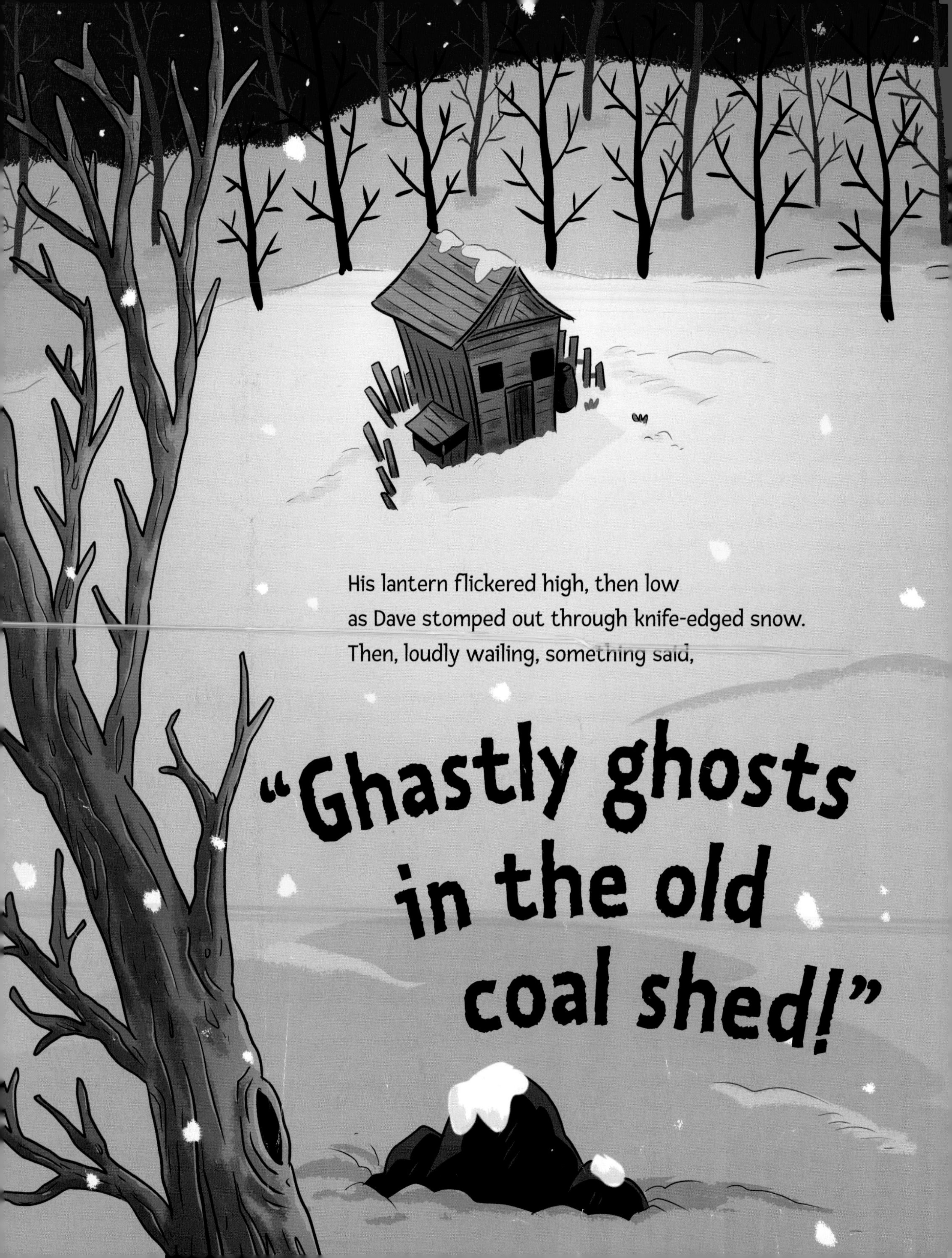

His lantern flickered high, then low
as Dave stomped out through knife-edged snow.
Then, loudly wailing, something said,

"Ghastly ghosts
in the old
coal shed!"

"Now cut that out!" Old Dave was firm.
"I'm not the type to quail nor squirm.
And though I'm not inclined to boast,
I fear neither ghoul nor ghost!"

It’s true Old Dave was brave and bold.
He needed coal to stop the cold.
But even brave men might think twice
when voices weave through wind and ice.
Old Dave gave out a hearty sneeze.
He had a choice—get coal, or freeze.

"I'll just pop in and do the job."
His wool-gloved hand reached for the knob.
He shivered and could barely speak.

The door swung open with a *CREEEAAAK.*

Then like cold thunder something said,

"Ghastly ghosts in the old coal shed!"

"THAT'S IT!" Dave roared. "I'VE HAD ENOUGH!
SO COME ON OUT. I CALL YOUR BLUFF!
IT'S COLD ENOUGH TO FREEZE MEN BLUE.
I HAVEN'T TIME TO WASTE ON YOU!"

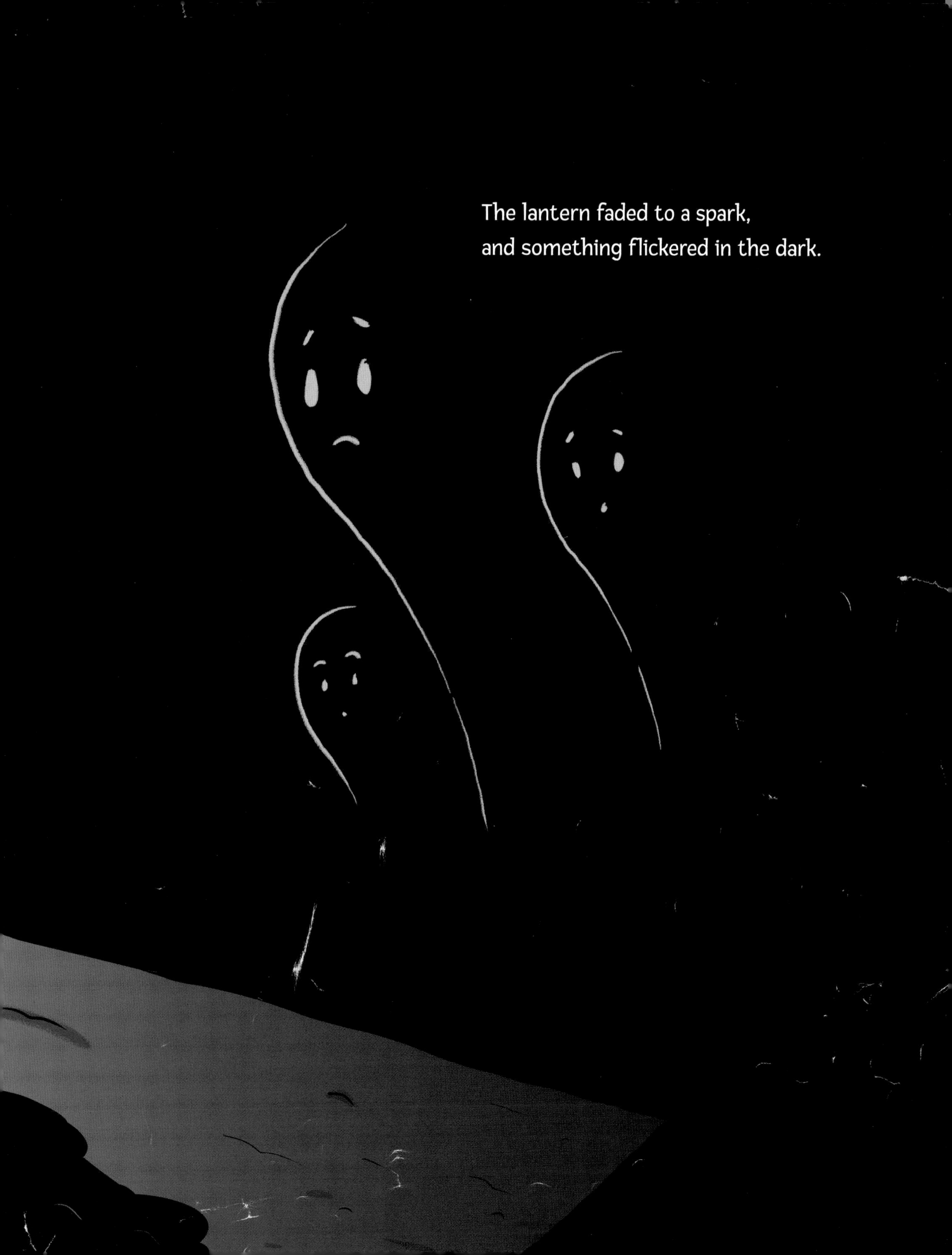

The lantern faded to a spark,
and something flickered in the dark.

"GHASTLY GHOSTS..."

"I know. I do. I'd like to bet you're cold ghosts too.
This night's not fit for man nor beast,
be he alive, or he deceased.
So rather than stay here and wail,
feel free to help me fill my pail."

"And then, before we *all* expire,
please come on up, and share my fire."

"GHASTLY GHOSTS…"

"And, by the way,
if you come to my house to stay,
you MUST find something ELSE to say!"

The wind dropped down.
Snow drifted white.
The moon began to light the night.
Dave heard a whispered groan:

"Allll riiiiiiight…"

Now Dave's got guests at his old place.
The ghosts don't take up too much space.
In fact, they're quite good company.
His friendless nights are history.

The cottage still sits on a height.
But lonely? Well, that's hardly right.
Warm windows glow. A fiddle's heard.
And from the coal shed?

Not

one

word.